This igloo book belongs to:

....

igloobooks

Published in 2017
by Igloo Books Ltd
Cottage Farm
Sywell
NN6 0BJ
www.igloobooks.com

Copyright © 2017 Hallmark Cards, Inc.

Illustrated by James Burks
Original story by Cat Skorupski

Cover designed by Nicholas Gage
Interiors designed by Helen Jones
Edited by Stephanie Moss

LEO002 0217
2 4 6 8 10 9 7 5 3 1
ISBN 978-1-78670-601-0

Printed and manufactured in China

Princess Millie's
Magic
Wand

igloobooks

Millie was walking along one day
when right before her eyes,
she saw a **sparkling**
wand and thought,
"**What a nice surprise!**"

Millie ran straight home and gave her magic wand a **wiggle**.

As soon as she made a wish, her baby sister...

... began to **giggle!**

"It works, yippee!" yelled Millie.

"My wish really came true!"

Then suddenly Millie thought,

"I wonder what else I could do?"

There was one thing Millie wanted, so she gave her wand a

swish!

She looked in the mirror and beamed.

She had got her princess wish.

"**Well done, wand!**" said Millie,
but she needed one more thing.
She couldn't wear a beautiful gown
without some princess **bling!**

ping-zing!

Suddenly a **sparkling** tiara appeared on Millie's head.

"Perfect! That's all the magic wishes I will ever need," she said.

But Millie's naughty brother laughed
and told her she looked silly.

"You're not a real princess," he said.
His teasing upset Millie.

So, Millie decided she would make just **one more** little wish.

She waved her wand and her brother became a green and **slimy** fish!

Suddenly, Millie's best friend, Polly, came **knocking** at the door.

"Polly, what's wrong?" asked Millie. "You've never looked so sad before!"

"My cat, Stripes, is missing,"
said Polly. "I don't know what to do."

"If anyone can help,"
said Polly, "I'm sure it will be you."

Millie didn't like to see her friend feeling so very sad.

She knew she needed a plan that was the **best** she'd ever had.

Millie knew being a royal princess had been **SO MUCH** fun for her.

But it couldn't last forever...

... things should be back as they were.

"I miss my comfy cap," said Millie,

"and my naughty little brother. I've had some lovely wishes...

... and now it's time for another."

Millie planned to change everything

back to how it was before.

Then she'd give her wand to Polly.

She knew she needed it more.

"Make a wish," said Millie. "Your cat will come home safe and sound."

Polly couldn't believe her ears. She was sure Stripes would never be found!

"Thank you, Millie!" called Polly,
as she raced away.
She smiled and
then turned back.

"You've really made my day!"

Then there was a **fizz** and a **sputter**, a **whizz** and a **zing!**

Poof!

Poof!

Millie's spells were all reversed. She said goodbye to her **bling!**

So Millie made a picnic,
her brother came along too.
"Here's your wand," said Polly.
"I'm giving it back to you!"

Millie's magic wand had
helped Polly find her cat.
So everyone was really happy,
and that was that!